TAYLOR-MADE TALES

THE PENGUIN'S PERIL

by

ELLEN MILES

AN
APPLE
PAPERBACK

SCHOLASTIC INC.
New York Toronto London Auckland Sydney
Mexico City Hong Kong New Delhi Buenos Aires

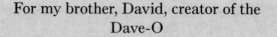

For my brother, David, creator of the
Dave-O

ISBN-13: 978-0-439-59711-1
ISBN-10: 0-439-59711-0

Title page art by Jonathan Bean
Book designed by Tim Hall

12 11 10 9 8 7 6 5 4 3 2 1   7 8 9 10 11 12/0

Printed in the U.S.A.   40

First printing, February 2007

Monday

Bacon. That was it! The perfect ingredient. Jason was sure of it. If he added a little bacon, his sandwich would have a nice, smoky flavor. But would it work with the onions? Jason tried to imagine how the flavors would taste together.

"Hmm," he said out loud.

"What?" asked Jennifer. She was looking through her backpack. Jason figured she was probably trying to find a pink barrette to match her sweatshirt. Jennifer liked her outfits to match. She and Jason were twins. They looked a lot alike, but they had totally different personalities. Jason never even gave a second *thought* to whether or not things matched. Getting dressed in the morning took him about two seconds. Basically, depending on the season, Jason would pull on a pair of jeans and then add Choice A: a basketball jersey or Choice B: a baseball T-shirt.

Today, Jason was wearing his Red Sox T-shirt, with number 24 on the back. (Manny Ramirez was Jason's favorite player.) Jason could just picture himself in a Red Sox uniform one day, swinging big and connecting hard for an inside-the-park home run. *Whap!* "Another incredible hit by Tourville!" the announcer would say as the crowd roared.

"Jason, *what*?" Jennifer repeated. "What are you 'hmm-ing' about?"

"Oh — nothing!" Jason waved a hand at Jennifer. They were sitting next to each other in their usual places in room 3B, waiting for their teacher, Mr. Taylor, to finish taking attendance. "Just thinking."

"I know." Jennifer grinned at him. "I can practically hear the gears turning. Bet I know what you're thinking about, too. The Amazin' Jason, am I right?"

"Shhh!" Jason frowned at her. Jennifer knew him too well. She knew that whenever he daydreamed, it was either about sports or food. And usually, it was food. Recipes, to be exact. Jason loved to eat, but he loved to cook even more. His favorite thing in the world — even more favorite than baseball or basketball or soccer — was making up new recipes.

But Jason wasn't exactly ready to tell the world about his love of food and cooking. It was sort of a secret thing, something he'd inherited from his dad. Moe Tourville had been in the restaurant business all his life. Now he was the owner and head chef of a little restaurant called J.J.'s, right on Main Street.

Jason wasn't sure how other kids would react if they knew he liked to cook. He figured it was better to keep it quiet. It just seemed *safer* to be famous for his curveball or three-point shot than for his lemon meringue pie or his clam chowder.

But Jennifer knew. She knew he loved to watch the Cooking Channel, and that he knew how to make a perfect omelette, and that he was on a never-ending quest to create the best sandwich of all time: the Amazin' Jason. He'd had the name picked out for years. It was the recipe that was taking a while.

Jennifer shrugged her shoulders. "Whatever," she said. She pulled a pink barrette out of her backpack and stuck it into her hair. "It's not like anybody's listening, anyway."

Jason had to admit that, as usual, Jennifer was right. Everybody else in class 3B was busy with something. Leo and Cricket were at the bulletin board, updating the "I Lost a Tooth!" chart. Oliver was feeding Guppyhead, the class fish. Molly was at her desk, concentrating on a drawing — probably of a horse, if Jason had to guess.

Still, it always paid to be safe. "Well, just keep it down, anyway," Jason said, frowning at his sister. Was it really such a good thing that their school allowed twins to be in the same class?

Just then, Mr. Taylor looked up from his attendance sheet.

"Good morning, kiddos." His bushy eyebrows wriggled up and down as he smiled around the room. "Happy Monday!"

Everybody groaned. Monday was not exactly their favorite day. Monday was math quiz day, for one thing. Mr. Taylor *tried* to make it fun. If you scored high, you got to go to the Treasure Chest and pick a prize: maybe a pencil sharpener in the shape of a dinosaur, or some scratch-and-sniff stickers. Still, the truth was that there was nothing fun about math quizzes.

Mr. Taylor frowned when he heard the groans. He thought for a second. "Would it be a happier Monday if we started a new tale today?"

This time, everybody cheered. Taylor-Made Tales were the *best*. How it worked was, you could give Mr. Taylor a list of any five items — anything you could imagine — and he would make a story out of them. Once he'd told the stories — he made them up out of thin air, it seemed — they got written down into the big red notebook that stayed on his desk.

Mr. Taylor had promised that everybody would get a turn to come up with the story elements, but so far he had never called on Jason. Still, Jason was always ready with his five items. They were good ones, too.

Up until now, nobody had come close to stumping Mr. Taylor. No matter how different the five items were, Mr. Taylor managed to fit them all into a story. But Jason had created the Ultimate Challenge: He had come up with five items that could not *possibly* be in the same story. It was like the opposite of making up a recipe where everything went together. What would Mr. Taylor do? Jason couldn't wait to find out.

Now Mr. Taylor was getting to his feet. "Sounds like you're all up for a story," he said. He stood and stretched his long arms. "So am I." He led the way over to the reading corner, where his big green chair was surrounded by a sea of colorful cushions. Jason ran to grab the red pillow. Red was his lucky color.

"Are we all settled?" Mr. Taylor asked after a moment. Then he looked around the circle of faces. His eyes met Jason's. "What'll it be, J.T.?"

The Ultimate Challenge

Whoa. It was finally his turn. For a second, Jason was too surprised to speak. Then he smiled a big, slow smile. "Okay. Ready?"

Mr. Taylor nodded. "Ready!"

Jason began. "A polar bear," he said.

Across the circle, Leo grinned. "That reminds me of a joke!" he said.

"Leo!" Jennifer was always impatient. "Not now!"

"Oh, go ahead, Leo," said Mr. Taylor. "We haven't had our joke of the day yet." Leo was the unofficial class comedian.

Leo stood up. "What did the polar bear eat after the dentist fixed its tooth?"

Nobody could guess.

"The dentist!" Leo laughed along with everybody else. Then he took a bow and sat down.

After everybody finished laughing, Mr. Taylor looked at Jason again. He raised his bushy eyebrows. "And?"

"And a penguin," Jason said, watching Mr. Taylor's face. That was the first part of the Ultimate Challenge. Jason — and everybody else in Mr. Taylor's class — knew that penguins only lived near the south pole and polar bears only lived up north, in the Arctic. They'd learned all about it just last month, when they were studying polar ecosystems.

Mr. Taylor nodded. Jason noticed that he didn't look nervous at all. But he still hadn't heard the rest of the Ultimate Challenge. "And some quicksand —" Jason was pretty sure that didn't exist at either polar region, "— and a cactus." Quicksand was in jungly areas, and cacti lived in deserts. Jason checked Mr. Taylor's face again to see if he was getting worried about how to put all these things together. But Mr. Taylor was just nodding.

Cricket stared at Jason. "Boy, you sure aren't making it easy," she said. "I figured you'd pick all sports stuff. Like a soccer field, or a hockey stick."

Jason grinned. "Well, my fifth item does have something to do with sports." He had thought about it for a long time, and realized that he just *had* to have something about the Red Sox in his story. And while he was at it, he might as well pick something really, really good. Something he wished and *wished* he owned. "My final item is a baseball signed by every single one of the 2004 Red Sox."

"Ah, yes. A World Series championship ball!" Mr. Taylor sounded admiring. "Well, of course we couldn't have left that out. It was Duncan's most treasured belonging."

"Who's Duncan?" asked Oliver.

"Duncan McTeagle." Mr. Taylor said, matter-of-factly. "You may not have heard of him, but you should have. He was one of the first American children to travel to — well, I guess you'll soon know all about it."

Jason couldn't believe it. Mr. Taylor was jumping right into the story, the way he always did. The Ultimate Challenge had not slowed him down one bit. Incredible. Jason shook his head as he watched Mr. Taylor reach up to turn on the light over his chair. The part of the lamp shade facing Jason glowed with streaks of purply reds and yellowish greens, the wild colors of the northern lights.

"Duncan followed behind Doc, stepping carefully into his father's big footprints," began Mr. Taylor, as he settled back in his chair and knit his long fingers together.

Doc (that's what everybody called Duncan McTeagle's father) had said there was no need to disturb the jungle underbrush any more than was necessary. Borneo was home to one of the world's richest ecosystems, and they were there to study the flora and fauna, not destroy it.

Well, actually they were there to fix a McTeagleometer, the device Duncan's dad had invented to measure . . . what? Duncan was never exactly sure, and Doc was never able to explain it without getting so technical that he lost Duncan after two sentences. But the thing was used by scientists studying the environment all over the globe, from Alaska to Zimbabwe. And Doc McTeagle

was the only one who knew how to calibrate it when it got out of whack. That meant that he and Duncan got to travel to — well, everywhere! In fact, that's what Duncan did instead of going to school. Doc always said that the *world* was Duncan's school. It was Doc's, too. He was an amateur naturalist as well as an inventor, and he loved to study his surroundings.

Last month they'd been in Ecuador. The month before that, Nepal. And now they were in the deepest, darkest, jungliest part of Borneo, one of the wildest places on earth. The air was thick, and Duncan was sweaty and hot as he and his father pushed their way through the thick green tangle of vines and trees. Duncan was hoping none of the vines were dangerous, like the ones with sticky, poisonous sap that he'd read about.

Suddenly, Doc stopped in his tracks. "Would you look at that?" He squatted down for a closer examination. They had emerged at the edge of a swamp, and the earth beneath them was muddy. Muddy enough that Duncan could clearly see a trail of pawprints. Doc bent to take a closer look.

"I do believe it's a binturong!" he said. "These tracks must be from last night, since — as you know — the binturong is a nocturnal hunter." He followed the tracks, groping in the side pocket of his tan safari jacket as he walked. He pulled out a small black notebook and flipped it open. "Oh, dear." Doc heaved a long sigh. "This is my geology notebook."

Keeping his eyes on the tracks, he rummaged in another pocket, pulled out an identical black notebook, and opened it. "Blasted Barometers! This one is for meteorological notes." He put it back and reached into a third pocket, on the back of his jacket. Doc had his jackets made by a tailor in Portugal who understood his need for lots of storage and carrying capacity. "Here we go!" He waved the notebook triumphantly. "Wildlife observations."

He pulled a leaky pen out of a fourth pocket and began to make notes as he was walking. "I recall from our studies that a young binturong can hang by its tail. Isn't that fascinating?" He and Duncan had read a great deal about Borneo in the weeks before their trip.

"Dad!" Duncan said.

Doc didn't seem to hear him. He began to scribble a sketch of the pawprint.

"Dad!" Duncan said again. "Watch out! That's quicksand!"

Quicksand

Yesss!" Jason said, pumping his fist. He had not expected the quicksand to come into the story quite so quickly, but he was happy to hear about it. Jason had always thought it would be really, really cool — though maybe a little bit scary — to be caught in quicksand.

Mr. Taylor barely paused in his storytelling. It was a good thing! Jason was dying to hear what happened next.

"What?" Doc whirled to face Duncan. "Did you say —" Suddenly, the part of his face that showed beneath his mosquito-netted hat (the bugs were fierce in Borneo) turned white. "Quicksand?" he finished weakly, as he watched his right foot — and then his right ankle and his right knee — disappear beneath the surface.

"Don't —" Duncan began.

"Help!" Doc began to thrash about wildly as he tried to pull his leg from the sucking sinkhole.

"— panic!" Duncan had to shout as loudly as he could to be heard over his father's yelling. "Don't panic!" he repeated. "Dad, I'm telling you, the worst thing you can do is —"

Doc thrashed around some more. "Help! Help!" He gasped for breath, and his face turned bright red. He held the little notebook high over his head, as if trying to save it from his own horrible fate.

"*Doc!*" Duncan spoke as firmly as he could. "Listen to me. I mean it."

Doc peered up at his son. By this time, the inventor was in up to both knees. "Okay," he said, in a small voice.

"And quit moving around," Duncan added. "You're only going to make it worse." Duncan was prepared for this. It had always been his job to read up on all the dangerous parts of any place he and Doc went — what poisonous snakes lived there; whether there might be a hurricane or a flood or a blizzard; whether they needed to get shots to prevent malaria, yellow fever, or some other nasty disease. There were times Duncan wished it was *Doc*'s job. After all, Doc was the dad. He should be the one protecting Duncan. But Doc's mind just didn't work that way. He was always looking at the bigger picture. Or — at a binturong pawprint. In any case, Duncan sometimes thought Doc was hopeless. Brilliant! Kind! Creative! But hopeless.

Borneo wasn't the first place Duncan and Doc had visited that had quicksand. Duncan had learned a long time ago that quicksand can occur almost anywhere there's enough water — and some sand. "Don't worry, it's just sand with a *lot* of water in it," he told Doc now. "You won't get sucked all the way down or anything."

"Well, that's certainly reassuring." Doc did not sound a whole lot calmer. Now he was in up to his hips.

"But the more you struggle," Duncan warned, "the faster you'll sink. You really just have to relax and let yourself float."

"Relax?" Doc raised an eyebrow. "Would *you* be able to relax?" Still, Duncan could see that his father was doing his best to follow his instructions. Doc had stopped grimacing and flailing around. But he was still holding his notebook high over his head. "Can you take this?" He waved it at Duncan.

Duncan took a half-step forward — then stopped himself. "No way!" He shook his head. "If I get sucked in, we'll *both* be in trouble."

"Good point." Doc managed to stick the notebook under his hat. Then he leaned back with a big sigh and let his body float on the sand. His legs began to rise to the surface.

"That's it!" Duncan tried to sound encouraging. "I've read that things float even better on quicksand than on water."

"Easy for you to say," Doc muttered, as he executed an extremely slow-motion backstroke out of the middle of the quicksand. "But," he added after a moment, "I can't deny that it's true." He smiled at Duncan. Then, with one last great effort, he hauled himself onto dry land. "Suffering Seismographs!" He scraped some quicksand off his boots. "Remind me never to do *that* again."

"Don't ever do that again," Duncan said, with a straight face.

"Thanks. I won't."

As it turned out, Duncan and Doc would not have to worry about quicksand for quite some time. When they finally made their way back to camp that evening, they found an urgent message waiting for Doc. It was from a scientific expedition. There was another McTeagleometer that needed his *immediate* attention.

That meant it was time for Duncan to start making plans. He was always in charge of making up the lists: what clothing they would need, how they would travel, what equipment to bring — all that stuff. Duncan sighed. Sometimes he wished he didn't have *quite* so much responsibility. But mostly, he didn't really mind taking care of the details. He knew Doc had many more important things to think about.

Still, this time the trip was going to take some extra planning.

This time they would be on their way to —

Just then, the bell rang. "Oops!" said Mr. Taylor,

glancing up at the clock. "I didn't realize how late it was. We'd better scramble or you'll be late for library time."

"Wait!" Jason couldn't believe it. Was he really going to stop now? "Can't you just tell us where they're going?"

Mr. Taylor smiled mischievously. "You'll find out soon enough." He turned off the light and unfolded his long, skinny body from the big green chair. "Now let's get moving, kiddos!"

You could always tell when Mr. Taylor had his mind made up. With a big sigh, Jason got up and went to find his library notebook.

Banished

All day, Jason kept hoping that Mr. Taylor would decide to tell some more of Duncan's story. There were times when Mr. Taylor would surprise the class that way, calling them over to the reading corner for another installment later in the afternoon. But naturally, just when the story was *really* getting interesting, this was not one of those days.

Jason was dying to know where the boy in the story — Duncan — and his father were going next. He kept looking over at the globe that sat on top of the encyclopedia bookcase. He especially looked at the two white areas at the top and bottom of the globe. He didn't think it would be the Arctic or Antarctic, because of the Ultimate Challenge. There were no polar bears in the Antarctic, no penguins in the Arctic. But he hoped it would be somewhere more exotic than, say, New Jersey. Would it be Australia? Maybe they were going to Norway. Jason had always wanted to go there, for some reason. He couldn't believe he was going to have to wait until the next day to find out.

He didn't know if Mr. Taylor was going to be able to conquer the Ultimate Challenge, but Jason did know one thing: This was going to be the best Taylor-Made Tale ever. He already felt like he knew Duncan and his father. In fact, he felt a little jealous of Duncan. Not just because he got to travel all over the world or because he didn't have to go to school. Jason was mainly jealous because Doc counted on Duncan for a lot. They were like a team.

"Duncan is so lucky," Jason said to Jennifer as they walked downtown together after school.

"Why?"

"Because his dad treats him like he's somebody who can *do* things. Not just a kid."

Jennifer shrugged. "I don't mind being a kid," she said. She stopped to look in the window of Rags, the new clothing store next door to J.J.'s. "I wonder if Dad and Mom would buy me those jeans."

Jason rolled his eyes as he watched his sister slip inside the store. Then he turned and pulled open the big double doors that led into J.J.'s. "Hey, Melissa." He waved to the waitress, who smiled at him as he ducked under the counter. "Hey, George." J.J.'s assistant cook was leaning over the big grill, flipping burgers with a spatula.

"Hey, chief! Your dad's in the back." George waved Jason over. "Hey, check this out!" He showed Jason a hamburger bun. "I ordered the ones with sesame seeds, like you suggested. You were right. They're much better."

Jason gave George a thumbs-up. Usually he would hang out by the grill for a while, chatting with George. But today he wanted to talk to his dad. He kept walking toward the back of the kitchen, where Moe Tourville was kneading dough for the crusty bread J.J.'s served with dinner.

"Hi, pal." Jason's dad looked up and smiled. "What's up? How was school?"

"School was okay." Jason examined the dough.

"Hey, can I do that?" He started to roll up his sleeves as he went over to the sink to wash his hands. Jason loved to knead bread.

"Not today, buddy," said his dad. "I'm kind of in a hurry, and —"

"If you're in a hurry, I can help!" Jason said. "Whatever you need, I can do it." It was true. Jason knew how to do almost anything George or his dad could do in the kitchen. He'd picked up a lot, hanging around. J.J.'s had been his second home for as long as he could remember.

"Jase, I know you can." His dad wiped his forehead with a floury hand, leaving a streak of white. "But it's a beautiful day out there. Go play baseball! We'll be fine."

Jason knew it was useless to argue. His dad didn't want him in the kitchen, that was clear. But he couldn't help mentioning his new idea for the Amazin' Jason. "Hey, Dad," he began. "Listen to this! *Bacon*. It's the perfect ingredient for my sandwich, don't you think?"

"Sure, sure." But Dad was looking over his shoulder, checking on the oven controls. Jason knew that the temperature should be set at 450 degrees for the bread, but he didn't say so. He just turned and left the kitchen.

"He doesn't mean anything by it," said Jason's mom when she found him moping on the sunporch at home. She didn't even have to be told what happened. She had guessed exactly why Jason had stomped up the stairs and flopped down on the couch. "Remember what I told you?"

"Yeah, yeah," Jason said. "All that stuff about how his dad made him work in the family restaurant, and he doesn't want me to give up my own dreams, blah, blah, blah."

"Jason." His mom's voice had that warning tone.

"Sorry," Jason said. "But doesn't he understand that I *like* to work at J.J.'s? That I'd rather cook than do anything?"

Mom sat down next to him and gave him a hug. "He just wants you to be happy."

Jason shook his head. If Dad wanted him to be happy, why was he banishing him from the one place he most wanted to be?

Packing Up

Mr. Taylor! Mr. Taylor!"

"Yes, Jennifer?"

"I bet I know where Duncan and Doc are going!"

"Do you, now?" Mr. Taylor looked interested. It was the next morning in class, and everyone was buzzing about Duncan's story.

Jason rolled his eyes. All through dinner at home the night before, Jennifer had been making wild guesses about Duncan's and Doc's destination. First she said it was Italy, because the Tourvilles were having spaghetti and meatballs. (*Excellent* meatballs. Jason had helped his mother make dinner. *She* never turned down his offers to help in the kitchen.) Then she guessed Finland. Jason didn't know why. Then it was Japan, New Zealand, and Mexico.

"Well, why don't we go over to the reading corner and get on with the story. Afterward, you can tell me if you were right." Mr. Taylor led the way. Everybody got settled in fast. They couldn't wait to find out what happened next to Duncan and his father.

Mr. Taylor didn't waste any time. He reached up and turned on the light, then took a deep breath and dove back into the story.

When Duncan woke up a few days later, he had a few strange moments when he couldn't quite figure out where he was. Instead of parrots and monkeys screaming to celebrate the rising sun, he was hearing sirens and car horns and shrieking brakes. The sounds of traffic. The sounds of — he finally figured it out — Boston. He and Doc had left Borneo. They were back in the United States, in the apartment they used as a home base between expeditions.

Then Duncan heard another noise: the tinkle of breaking glass. "Great Geiger Counters!" he heard his father say. Even though it was early, Doc was already hard at work in the little room off the kitchen, the place he called his "inventorium." He spent every possible minute in there when they were home, working on inventions. Also — since he was Doc — breaking things, spilling things, and even occasionally blowing things up.

Duncan groaned and rolled over, pulling a pillow over his head. It was going to be a busy day. They had a plane to catch that afternoon, and Duncan had three to-do lists to work his way through before they left for the airport. Plus, he had to open up their basement storage cabinet and get out their cold-weather gear. They were going to need their warmest parkas, mittens, and boots for this trip.

"I knew it!" Jennifer shouted. "Finland, right?"

"Close," said Mr. Taylor. "They're going just a little farther north."

Jennifer looked at the globe. "But what's north of Finland?" she asked.

"Not much," admitted Mr. Taylor. "Mostly just a whole lot of ice. And — the North Pole."

"Cool!" Jason burst out. "They're going to the North Pole?"

Mr. Taylor nodded. "If I ever get them out of Boston, that is," he said with a smile. "Should I go on?"

"Definitely!" Jason leaned back on his cushion. He couldn't wait to find out how Mr. Taylor was going to work a penguin into a story about the North Pole.

By the time Duncan got up, he found Doc in the kitchen, cracking eggs into a skillet. "Sunny-side up?" Doc asked. He was a pretty good cook, as long as he didn't get interested in something else and forget that the stove was on.

After breakfast, Doc headed back into his inventorium and Duncan got to work on his lists. By mid-morning, the living room rug was completely covered with clothing and gear, and Duncan was standing in the middle of it all, scratching his head. By noon, everything was packed into an array of suitcases, backpacks, and duffel bags. And by two o'clock, the time Duncan had decided they *really* needed to be heading out, he was just scratching the last item — "Ask T. T. to water plants" — off his last to-do list. He'd already written out the note that he planned to leave under their neighbor's door.

"Ready?" he asked Doc. "The taxi will be here any second."

Doc shoved a few tools into his carry-on bag. "Ready! All we have to do now is pick up Pete."

"Pete?" Duncan stared at his father. "Who's Pete?"

"Didn't I tell you?" Doc asked. "I was sure I had. Oh, well. I'm telling you now. My old friend Pete is coming along on our expedition. I always promised him that if I went to the North Pole, he could come, too. We're picking him up on the way to the airport."

Duncan sighed. It wasn't the first time his father had made arrangements without telling him. "Okay," he said. "But I hope Pete's ready to go. We don't have a lot of extra time to waste."

"He'll be ready." Doc was confident. "I called his keeper this morning."

Meet Pete

Keeper?" Jason gave Mr. Taylor a curious look. "What do you mean, *keeper*?"

"That's exactly what Duncan was wondering," Mr. Taylor said.

Doc asked the taxicab driver to pull up in front of the big, wrought-iron gates. "Dad?" Duncan squinted at the sign. "Mind telling me what we're doing at the zoo?"

"Picking up Pete," said Doc. "Like I told you." He jumped out of the cab and asked the driver to wait. Then he strode in through the gates and disappeared, only to reappear a few moments later pulling a little red wagon. On the wagon was a small dog-carrier, the kind that has a screened window on one end and a handle on top.

Duncan was mystified. He got out of the cab and walked over to meet his dad. He stooped to look inside and caught a flash of something sleek and black-and-white. A puppy? No, not with that funny beak. Duncan could hardly believe he was seeing what he *thought* he was seeing. "Dad, what's in there?"

"Not *what*," Doc corrected him. "*Who*. This is Pete."

There was a loud squawk from the carrier.

"But —" Duncan stood up straight and stared at his father. "Pete is a *penguin*."

Doc nodded. "An Adélie penguin, to be exact. There are thousands of them in Antarctica. But Pete's one of a kind. Didn't I ever tell you the story of how Pete and I met?"

"Uh, no." Duncan shook his head. "I'm pretty sure I would remember that."

"Help me get him into the cab, and I'll tell you on the way to the airport." Doc bent to lift the carrier.

Pete squawked a few more times as Doc and Duncan lifted the dog-carrier into the backseat of the cab.

The driver pretzeled around and peered into the

carrier. "Hey, I'm not so sure I want that weird bird inside the car!"

"Pete is very quiet," Doc assured the man. "And very tidy. We'll be out of your hair in about ten minutes, as soon as you drop us at the airport."

The driver sighed. "Oh, all right."

Duncan dug in his pockets, looking for an extra dollar to add to the man's tip. "So?" he asked Doc, once they were moving again.

"Pete adopted me about eight years ago," said Doc. "When I was on a job down in Antarctica. He was just a chick, and I guess he had lost his own parents. He kind of — imprinted on me. You know, the way baby geese do? Whoever they see first when they hatch, they'll follow around forever. Basically, Pete thinks I'm his mother."

Duncan was quiet for a moment, thinking about his own mother, who was still alive back then, when Doc returned from Antarctica with a penguin. Duncan didn't remember that time at all. Or did he? Something about Pete's squawk did seem sort of familiar. And he could almost picture a penguin pacing the kitchen floor. But it was more like a dream than a memory. "What did Mom say when you brought him home?"

"Well, let's just say that she convinced me that he belonged at the zoo." Doc sounded sheepish. "And she was right. He made an awful mess of the bathroom during the few days he lived in our tub." He smiled fondly, remembering. "But I have always thought that it would be interesting to see how a penguin would survive in the Arctic. After all, the environments are very similar. It's a bit of a mystery why there aren't any penguins up there."

"So that's what you meant about promising Pete you'd take him if you ever went to the North Pole?" Duncan asked.

Doc nodded. "I can't believe we're finally going there!" He patted the top of Pete's box, which made Pete squawk. "I hope he likes it."

"Now wait just a minute," Oliver burst out. He was frowning as he pushed his glasses up his nose. He glared at Mr. Taylor. "That can't be true. Nobody would let you take a penguin out of Antarctica. They're a protected species, right? And it's not like you can just bring a penguin up to the North Pole. There would be laws about that!" Oliver always took things very seriously. "Plus, do baby penguins really act like baby geese and follow somebody around? Imprinting? I've never heard of that."

Mr. Taylor just nodded and smiled. "You're probably right," he said. "I'm just telling the story the way I heard it. I never promised that every word in every one of my stories would be the complete and total truth."

"Yeah!" Jennifer shook back her hair. "That's why they call them *stories*, right?" Jason noticed that his sister seemed to have forgotten how suspicious she had been when Mr. Taylor told them the very first tale, which was about a dog who learned to talk.

"I suppose you're right, Jennifer," said Mr. Taylor. Jason thought he was hiding a smile. "Now, shall I go on?"

It wasn't hard getting Pete onto the plane. The flight attendant seemed to think they had a small dog inside their carrier, and Duncan and Doc let her believe what she wanted to. The flight went smoothly, except for one moment when there was a lot of turbulence and the plane bounced around a bit. Pete let out a squawk that did *not* sound as if it could possibly have come from a dog. But Doc covered up with a fake coughing fit, and nobody seemed the wiser.

The flight went smoothly — that is, until they neared their destination, a tiny Arctic village not far from the base camp where the other members of their polar expedition were waiting to meet them. That was when the voice of the pilot came over the loudspeaker. "Folks, I'm sorry to have to tell you this, but we're not going to be able to land. It's blowing and snowing, and we have zero visibility."

There were groans throughout the cabin of the plane.

"But don't worry," the pilot went on. "We have a ship waiting near another airport where we *can* touch down, and it'll just be a short voyage from there."

Duncan was relieved. Their travel plans were *already* pretty complicated, without weather fouling things up. That was the problem with traveling in the Arctic: Weather almost *always* fouled things up. You only had a small window of opportunity for travel — in the spring. That was when the ice was still firm enough so that you could move safely over it, but the days were longer and the temperatures were a little warmer. And even in spring, the weather was very unpredictable.

The plane landed easily, and Duncan and Doc — and Pete, in the carrier — soon boarded the boat. It was a big, old rusty freight ship with a crew that seemed to speak nothing but Russian. The ship set sail through choppy seas almost immediately. Duncan did not feel at all well as the ship lurched and tossed. That night, he rolled back and forth in his bunk and didn't sleep a wink. It didn't help that he kept hearing Pete rolling back and forth, too. And that every time Pete rolled, he squawked. And that every time Pete squawked, Doc called out, "It's okay, Pete!"

What about, "It's okay, Duncan?" Duncan thought Doc seemed more concerned about Pete than he did about his own son. Was it crazy to be jealous of a penguin? But it was probably just the lack of sleep that was making Duncan think that way.

Then, in the morning, there was some more bad news.

"Ice," said the burly, bearded captain of the ship when he approached Duncan and Doc. They had given up on sleep and were out on deck, leaning over the railing. The ship was still rolling, and their faces were practically green. Pete was out of his carrier. He stood close to Doc, staring down into the water. If a penguin's face could look green, Pete's definitely did. He kept squawking as he looked back and forth from the waves to Doc's face, as if asking, "What's going on here?"

The captain gestured toward a far-off shoreline, then helplessly down at the surging sea ice that surrounded the ship. "Ice," he repeated. "We no can go." It wasn't a sheet of unbroken ice — in fact, Duncan saw little creeks of open water threading all through it — but it was thick enough to make it nearly impossible for the big ship to push through.

The captain's face brightened. "But they will

take you!" He pointed to a sprinkling of black specks that was drawing closer — and getting bigger — by the minute.

Soon, Duncan could see that the specks were actually small boats, just big enough for one or two people. "Look!" he shouted. He hadn't had a lot of time to read up on the Arctic, but he'd heard of the native Inuit people and of their low-riding canoes. They were called *kayaks*, and they were perfect for moving through the *leads*, the channels of open water in the sea ice.

Doc patted the pockets of his puffy down parka, searching for a notebook. "Fascinating," he muttered as the boats drew closer. Pete stood on tiptoe to stare over the railing. He let out a soft, questioning squawk. "That's right, Pete. Kayaks." Doc patted the penguin's sleek black head.

Meanwhile, the captain was lowering a long rope ladder down the tall, rusty side of the ship. Duncan gulped. That icy, black water looked awfully cold!

"Leaping Logarithms! How am I going to get

down there carrying Pete *and* my tools?" Doc asked.

"You take the tools," Duncan suggested. "I'll take Pete."

Pete squawked. It sounded like, "WHAT????" Duncan could tell that the little penguin did not like the idea of being separated from Doc.

"I know, I know," said Doc, giving Pete a pat. "But we'll be together again as soon as we reach shore." He shouldered his backpack of tools and began to climb gingerly down the ladder.

With another loud squawk, Pete slid toward the railing. Before Duncan could grab him, the penguin jumped off the deck and landed right smack on top of Doc's backpack. "Whoa!" yelled Doc, as he teetered on the ladder. It looked like he and Pete were both going to fall into the choppy, frigid waves!

Jason Gets Caught

When the bell rang and Mr. Taylor stopped speaking, nobody said a word. It was as if they were all bewitched. What an awesome story!

All day, Jason thought about Duncan and Doc and Pete and their incredible trip. He could hardly wait to hear what happened next. Were Pete and Doc going to plunge into the icy sea? But once again, Mr. Taylor let the whole day go by without even *suggesting* more story time.

"Going to J.J.'s?" Jennifer asked as she and Jason left school that afternoon.

Jason shook his head. "Dad'll just chase me away."

"I heard there's a baseball game at Deakins field." Jennifer swung her bookbag. "Leo told me. He said they really need a pitcher."

Jason shrugged. He couldn't say why, exactly,

but he just didn't feel like playing baseball. "I'm going downtown to the library," he told Jennifer. He wanted to find some books about expeditions to the North Pole. The school library only had two, and they were both checked out.

Jennifer made a face. "The library? Boring! I'm meeting Chelsea at the Purple Daisy." That was a store downtown that sold earrings and hair ties and stuff. Jason had never set foot inside it, and he intended to keep it that way.

The library was crowded when Jason walked in. There were teenagers working at the computers, kids reading in the corners, and a line of people waiting to check out books. Jason found a free computer and typed in "North Pole," and "Arctic Travel." He wrote down the numbers for some of the books that sounded good. Then he brought his paper to the librarian at the desk. "Can you help me find these?" he asked.

"Sure!" She smiled at him and put down her pen. "Follow me." She led him into a big room where there were lots of rows of bookshelves. "These books will be in the nonfiction area," she said, "because they are true stories about a real place."

Jason knew that. He just didn't know how to find the particular books he wanted. He didn't like being treated like a little kid, but he knew the librarian didn't mean to insult him. "Thanks," was all he said when she pointed out a shelf of books on the Arctic.

"Cool subject!" She said, adding a little laugh to show it was a joke.

Jason laughed, too. Then he pulled a bunch of books off the shelf and sat down to look them over. He ended up sitting there for a long time, reading about different kinds of snow and ice, ways of living in the cold, and the types of animals that thrived in the Arctic. Jason read about Admiral Peary, who led the first successful expedition to the North Pole in 1909, and Will Steger, who traveled there by dog sled in 1986. He read about the Inuit people and their way of life, and even found a great diagram of a kayak, showing how it was made by stretching sealskin over walrus bones. The Inuits were amazing hunters, and they always used every part of the animals they killed.

Jason was so lost in the books that he was surprised when he glanced up at the clock and saw that it was almost five o'clock. He had promised to help his mom make enchiladas that night, and it was time to head home. Jason chose three books he wanted to take out and headed for the checkout desk. But on the way there, he saw something that distracted him.

Cookbooks. A whole row of them.

Jason had forgotten that the library had cookbooks. He usually just used the ones his dad had collected over the years. But here were a whole bunch he had never seen before. There was one on Greek cooking, and one about how to decorate beautiful cakes. Jason put down his Arctic books and started to pull cookbooks off the shelf. *A Hundred and One Chicken Recipes*! *The Louisiana Cookbook*! *The Joy of Cooking*! *Barbecue and More*! Jason was in heaven as he paged through the books, looking at the mouthwatering pictures.

Jason could never understand why some people thought cooking was hard. The truth was, it was easy. If you knew how to read and you could follow directions, you could cook *anything*! That was the coolest thing. If Jason decided he wanted to make Tournedos Rossini — whatever that was — he could! Once he had a recipe, all he needed was the right ingredients, the right equipment, and some free time.

Jason grabbed three cookbooks and added them to the stack of books he was taking out. He could hardly wait to take them home and read through them more carefully.

"Find everything you need?" the librarian asked as she stamped his books.

Jason nodded. "Yup! Thanks." He picked up the tall stack and headed out the door.

"Hey, you! Bookworm!" Somebody was yelling at him.

Jason turned to see Daniel, one of the fifth-graders who organized the baseball games at Deakins field. "Hey," Jason said.

"Where *were* you today?" Another fifth-grader,

Justin, was walking with Daniel. He was carrying a mitt. "We could've used your arm."

"I had a report to do." Jason knew it wouldn't be cool to admit going to the library just because he wanted to.

"Yeah? What about?" Daniel took a step closer to look at the books Jason was carrying. "Hey! What's this?" He grabbed one off the top of the pile. "*Lovely Cakes You Can Make*!" He flashed the book at Justin. The pink cake on the cover seemed to shimmer and glow in the sunlight.

Justin cracked up. "Ooh," he said. "Where's your apron, Betty Crocker?"

Jason felt his stomach clench up. This was *exactly* why he didn't tell people he liked to cook. He felt his face get hot, and he knew he was blushing. He hated that. Without saying a word, he grabbed the book and stuck it on his pile. Then he started to walk again, as quickly as he could.

"Sensitive, huh?" he heard Justin say to Daniel.

Both boys snickered.

Jason gulped. He knew he was going to be hearing more about this.

Trouble

It started first thing the next morning, about two milliseconds after Jason arrived on the playground. The usual kickball game was already in full swing. Just about every kid from grades three, four, and five joined in the daily game. It began before the first bell, continued at recess, and often went on after school ended. Nobody really kept score, but everybody knew who the best players were.

Jason was one of them.

So was Justin. Daniel, too.

There were also plenty of girls who could kick home runs or field hard grounders. But Jennifer was not one of them. She hated how the kickball field was always so dusty.

"Tourville!" A kid named Dennis waved Jason over as soon as he stepped foot on the field. "You're on our team. Come on. You're up next."

Jason saw Justin and Daniel out in the field. Justin was pitching, and Daniel was playing first. Jason hesitated.

"Hurry up! Put your stuff over there." Dennis pointed to a pile of jackets and backpacks. Jason sighed and threw his bookbag on the pile. Then he got in line behind home base.

The boy who was up before him kicked a hard one to center field and ran to first.

Jason took his place at home base and stood, waiting for a pitch.

"Hey, Tourville!" yelled Daniel, from first base. "What's for dinner?"

On the pitcher's mound, Justin smirked. "Ready for a meatball — I mean, *groundball*?"

Jason knew he had to just ignore them. If he didn't, they would tease him even more. "Yeah, I'm ready! Bring it on!"

"Bring *what* on?" Justin asked. "A lovely pink cake?" He looked around to see if anybody got the joke. A few kids were laughing.

Jason gulped. That meant that Justin and Daniel had already spread the word. He wanted to walk away from the field and hide in the boys' room until the first bell rang. But he knew that would be a huge mistake. Instead, he just waited for the laughter to end. And when Justin finally rolled the ball toward him, Jason kicked it so hard and so high that it soared right over the slide and almost hit some kindergartners on the teeter-totter.

Jason's team went wild as he circled the bases.

A few minutes later, the bell rang and the torture was over. But as Jason ran for the school's side door with everyone else, Justin and Daniel caught up with him. "Have a great day, cupcake!" said Justin. Daniel cracked up.

When he got to room 3B, Jason plopped down in his chair and let out a big sigh. Mr. Taylor looked up from his desk. "Something wrong, J.T.?" he asked.

Jason shook his head. Something *was* wrong, but there was nothing Mr. Taylor could do. Except . . . "Can you tell us what happened next to Duncan and Doc?" he asked.

"I'd be happy to." Mr. Taylor still looked concerned. But he didn't bug Jason. He just waited until everybody was in class, then herded them all over to the reading corner for another installment of Duncan's story.

"Pete!" Duncan yelled. He couldn't believe that the silly little penguin had jumped off the ship and onto Doc's backpack.

"What do I do?" Doc shouted helplessly as he dangled from the ladder, doing his best to hold on.

"Don't move!" Duncan was worried that if Doc tried to climb back up, Pete would fall off. Duncan lay down on the deck and leaned out as far as he could, stretching his arms down to try to reach Pete. Almost! But not quite. Duncan turned to look up at the ship's captain. "Hold my feet!"

With his feet secure, Duncan squirmed his body out so that he could lean down even further. He managed to grab Pete by the back of his neck. "Squawk all you want," he told the black-and-white bird. "You're coming back up."

Pete *did* squawk, but Duncan managed to haul him up on deck. "You listen to me," he said, once the penguin was safe. "I know you want to be with Doc. But sometimes you just can't. And that's that."

"Is he okay?" Doc called from the ladder.

"He's fine." Duncan noticed that Doc didn't seem worried about *him*. He rubbed his arm. It was sore from stretching it so far. But the main thing was that everyone was safe. He gave Pete a quick hug. The little dope.

Doc finished climbing down the ladder, and slipped into the second cockpit of a double kayak paddled by one of the Inuit men. "It's not so hard!" he yelled back up.

On deck, Pete let out a frightened squawk as Duncan helped him climb inside the backpack one of the sailors had offered. "I know," Duncan said. "I'm a little scared, too." He shouldered the back-pack and swung himself over the railing. Slowly, carefully, he made his way down the rope ladder as the waves beneath showered him with cold, salty spray. Another kayak was waiting, and Duncan climbed into it, sighing with relief once he was off the ladder.

"Interesting pet," said the man piloting the kayak.

"That's Pete." Then Duncan realized the man had probably never seen anything like Pete before, not up here near the North Pole. "He's a penguin."

"Yup, seen 'em on the Internet. I'm Robert Tulugaq," said the man. "Don't worry, we'll get you to where you're going." He started to paddle off through the choppy, ice-strewn seas.

Duncan could feel Pete squirming around in the backpack. "Hang in there, buddy," he said. There was barely room for Duncan in the kayak's little cockpit. Pete was going to have to ride inside the backpack for now. "You'll be safer if you stay still."

Pete settled down after a while as Robert expertly piloted the kayak through the channels of open water. "Isn't this is a wonderful experience?" Doc shouted from his kayak. He had one of his little notebooks out, and he was scribbling observations.

"Wonderful," Duncan agreed. "As long as we don't drown."

"Or get swallowed up by one of those," Robert said calmly, pointing his paddle at a huge, sleek, white-and-black body that had just surfaced about ten feet away. The creature was bigger — *much* bigger — than the kayak.

"Yikes!" shouted Duncan. "Isn't that a killer whale?" According to his reading, killer whales — or orcas, as they were known — rarely actually attacked humans. But they loved to eat seals — and penguins! Orcas could be found all over the world, in Antarctica as well as the Arctic.

Robert nodded calmly. "Orcas don't usually show up until a little later in the spring," he said. "This fellow is here early." He steered the kayak away from the beast.

Smoothly and silently, the orca switched direction and began to follow the kayak.

Inside his backpack, Pete squawked and squirmed. Then, suddenly, Duncan heard a splash. "Pete!"

"Jumping Juggernauts!" Doc shouted, as Pete landed in the water.

The orca circled closer.

Mush!

What do we do?" *Duncan stared in horror as* Pete began to swim as hard as his little black-and-white wings could swim — away from the orca and straight toward Doc's kayak. Pete must have decided he just *had* to be closer to Doc. The plump little bird squirted through the water, swimming more gracefully than Duncan would have imagined. He was fast, too — but not fast enough. The orca had turned again and was closing in on the penguin. The killer whale's mouth yawned wide, showing off rows of sharp white teeth against a huge pink tongue. Duncan could almost imagine that the orca was licking its lips in anticipation of a little penguin snack. "Pete!" he yelled again. This penguin was a pain in the neck. He was going to get them all killed.

"Hold tight!" Robert shouted. He paddled about

ten hard, strong strokes, then shifted his weight. The kayak leaned hard toward the right, and Robert reached out a hand to grab Pete by the scruff of his neck. He pulled him close and popped the little bird right inside his cockpit, where the orca couldn't see him. "Safe now," Robert said, steadying the rocking boat.

By then, the other kayak had drawn closer. "How can I ever thank you, Mr. Toolaroo?" Doc asked.

"It's Tulugaq. Means Raven. And you don't have to thank me. I understand that this little penguin is important to you. Orca can find something else to eat."

"Well, I *do* thank you. And I'm sure Pete does, too."

When he heard Doc say his name, Pete let out a squawk that echoed inside the cockpit. Everybody laughed. Maybe the worst was over.

Then Duncan heard something else. "What's that sound?" What a racket! He looked overhead, expecting to see a huge V of geese flying by, honking their heads off.

Robert glanced back at Duncan and smiled. "That's just the dogs barking," he said. "Elmer and Freddie and Tractor and Vera and Roxy. And about six others. They belong to my cousin, Stan. They can't wait to meet you!" He paddled hard and the kayak slid past a tall iceberg. Suddenly, Duncan could see that they were nearing shore.

"Land!" he said.

Robert shook his head. "Ice," he answered. "There is no land this far north. Only ice. But no more open water. The kayaks cannot go farther. Now you'll travel by dogsled."

"Really?" Duncan felt his heart thump hard. This *was* an adventure. He had ridden on an elephant once, and he had flown in a hot-air balloon, but he had never been pulled by a pack of barking dogs.

And boy, did they bark! They barked the whole time as Robert pulled his kayak up to the ice and helped Duncan out. They barked at Doc, too. And they barked even more loudly at Pete when he emerged from Robert's cockpit and waddled as fast as he could toward Doc.

Doc swept Pete into his arms. "It's okay, little fella," he said. "You'll be safe. I won't let the dogs bite you."

Pete nestled his head into Doc's shoulder and closed his eyes tightly, as if what he couldn't see couldn't hurt him. Duncan was a little nervous about the dogs, too, and he wouldn't have minded getting a hug like that. But he knew he wasn't a little kid anymore — even though there were times he wished he were.

Robert introduced Duncan and Doc to his cousin, Stan. "Okay, then," he said. "Have a good trip, now!" He and the other man jumped back into their kayaks and paddled off before Duncan could say a word.

"Hop in!" Stan had to yell to be heard over the dogs. They were barking like crazy, and jumping up and down. "They can't wait to get going," Stan shouted. "These dogs live to pull!"

Duncan and Doc tucked their luggage into the big wooden sled that was attached to the dogs by a long line. Then Doc, who had Pete cozied up inside his jacket, climbed aboard and stuck out a hand for Duncan. Duncan had barely found a spot to squeeze into when Stan yelled "Hup-hup-hup!" and the dogs took off. They ran at top speed over the smooth, frozen surface that seemed to spread for miles around, for as far as Duncan could see. The snow was blindingly white, and the sky was a brilliant blue, and the barking of the dogs rang out in the cold, clear air.

"They're a great team!" Stan yelled. "Roxy is the smartest, strongest lead dog I've ever worked with!" He was running alongside the sled, panting big frosty puffs of air as he spoke. "Brave, too! She faced down a polar bear last week."

Duncan felt his whole body go hot, then cold. "Polar bear?" he asked. "They have polar bears around here?"

"Magnificent Mammoth Mammalians!" Doc rummaged for his wildlife notebook. "I've always been intrigued by huge, predatory beasts." Pete snuggled closer to Doc, as if the words frightened him.

Stan raised an eyebrow. "I'm sure they'd find you pretty fascinating, too. And you'd make a delicious snack, to boot."

Doc just laughed, but Duncan's mouth felt dry. He did not like the idea of running into a huge, white, hungry bear.

"Don't worry!" Stan must have seen the fear on Duncan's face. He patted a rifle that was stuck into the side of the sled. "Tranquilizer darts," he explained. "Stops 'em in their tracks."

"Great." Duncan hoped he would never have to test out that trick.

"No bears today," Stanley said. "Here we are at base camp." Sure enough, Duncan suddenly saw a cluster of brightly colored tents scattered on the ice just ahead of them.

"Base camp?" Duncan asked. "How much farther is it to the North Pole?"

"Oh, it's still quite a way," Stan said, as he slowed down the team. "You'll rest up here, then dog-team north for another few days."

Duncan was suddenly very tired. He was cold, too. The biting Arctic wind had worked its way through his thick parka, and his eyelashes were frozen solid. He was so sleepy that he barely made it through the introductions as he and Doc met the team that would accompany them to the top of the world. All Duncan remembered was a bunch of bearded guys with glasses, plus a few women with sunburned faces and their hair in braids.

They ate dinner in the mess tent — freeze-dried mashed potatoes and some kind of meat (they didn't have many fresh vegetables way up there on the ice, not that Duncan missed broccoli). Afterward, a nice lady in a red parka showed Duncan, Doc, and Pete to the supply tent. There were three cots wedged between the piles of boxes in the tent, one large one for Doc and two smaller ones for Pete and Duncan.

Before he collapsed onto his cot, Duncan dug into his backpack to find the one thing he always kept very near, no matter where in the world he was sleeping. It was his most prized possession, something that reminded him of home and of his mother, who had always been the one to take him to baseball games. She had given Duncan this special gift on his birthday, just a month before she had died.

It was a baseball. But not just *any* baseball. This

one had been used in the 2004 World Series. And it was signed by every single member of the winning team: the Boston Red Sox.

Pete climbed down off his cot near Doc's and waddled over to get a closer look. He tilted his head back and forth as he examined the ball. He let out a questioning squawk.

"Yup," Duncan said. "It's the real thing, all right."

Pete seemed satisfied with that answer, and after another long look at the ball, he waddled back to his cot.

Duncan closed his eyes and took a big sniff of the heavy little ball. It smelled like summer, and green grass, and leather. Then, as he did almost every night before going to sleep, Duncan started reading the names on the ball. Trot Nixon. Manny Ramirez. Jason Varitek. Going through those familiar names always made him feel like everything was going to be all right. But before he even got to Pedro Martinez, he fell asleep, still clutching the ball.

Duncan slept hard, and he slept for a long time.

When he woke up the next morning, the tent was empty.

Doc was already gone.

So was Pete.

And so was the baseball.

Lost . . . and Found

No way!" Jason could hardly stand it. No sooner had the ball made an appearance than it had disappeared! "He *can't* have lost that ball."

If you had told Jason that someday he could be jealous of a character in a story, he wouldn't have believed you. But Mr. Taylor made the stories seem so real, even when they were about things that couldn't *really* have happened. So Jason did envy Duncan. Not only did the guy get to plan — and *go* on — expeditions, he also owned the one item in the universe that Jason would have prized over all others. And now it was gone!

"I didn't say he lost it," Mr. Taylor said mildly. "I just said it wasn't in the tent when he woke up."

"But who could have taken it?" Jason was

baffled. "I mean, they're not exactly in a high-crime neighborhood up there."

Next to him, Leo nodded. "I know. What would an orca want with a Red Sox ball?" He scratched his head. Jason had the feeling Leo was about to make a joke. Leo's jokes were usually pretty funny, but right now Jason just wanted Mr. Taylor to go on with the story.

"So?" Jason asked. "Where was the ball?"

"That's what Duncan was wondering," said Mr. Taylor.

Duncan searched everywhere. Under the cots. Between the boxes marked "beef jerky" and "toe warmers." Behind the piles of ice drills and snow shovels and ski poles. The ball was nowhere to be found.

Duncan ran to the breakfast tent. "Dad!" he said. "My ball! Have you seen it?"

Doc was in the middle of explaining his latest invention to the team communications officer. "You see," he was saying, "when the sound waves travel through this pseudocrystalline substance . . ." He turned to look at Duncan. "Ball?" He shook his head. "What ball?"

Duncan rolled his eyes. "Never mind. Where's Pete?"

"Pete's missing?" Now Doc looked a little more concerned. But clearly, his mind was on pseudo-crystalline substances. There would be *no* talking to him.

Duncan ran back outside, forgetting that he hadn't zipped up his parka yet. "Brrr!" It must have been thirty below out there! He felt the little hairs inside his nose freeze as he took a deep breath. "Pete!" he shouted. "Where are you?" He listened hard for an answering squawk. Nothing. But then his eye caught a flash of black against the white. It was Pete! The penguin was just disappearing into the mess tent.

Duncan dashed over and pushed aside the flap. The tent was deliciously warm and smelled of bacon and eggs. Duncan's stomach rumbled, but breakfast was the last thing on his mind. He followed Pete's waddling figure right into the kitchen area. "Ha! Back already?" Dave the cook was saying to Pete. "You want *more*? Okay!" He reached into a jar and pulled out a handful of shiny dried black beans. Pete squawked and stretched his neck out when he saw them.

"I don't know what you're doing with these, but you're welcome to them. The crew is sick of beans." Dave put the beans on the floor of the tent, and Pete bent to pick several up in his bill.

Duncan's eyes narrowed. He knew *just* what Pete was doing with those beans. He probably thought they were little pebbles. Penguins, Duncan had read, built their *nests* out of pebbles. And both male and female penguins took care of the precious eggs that were laid on those nests.

Duncan slipped behind a tentpole as Pete waddled by, his beak full of beans. Then, as Pete passed, Duncan followed him. Through the tent. Out the door. Around to the back, to where there was a sheltered area between two sleeping tents.

Pete waddled proudly, carrying his beakful of

beans. And then, as Duncan watched, the penguin bent, and nudged the beans carefully into place. . . .

Around a World Series championship baseball, signed by each one of the Red Sox.

Home Run

Batter, batter, batter!"

"Go, team!"

"Watch out! Leo's about to steal second!"

Jason let the familiar shouts wash over him. After school, he had decided to celebrate the fact that Duncan had found his ball by playing some baseball himself. He shook his head, smiling to himself. Pretty funny that a penguin would mistake a baseball for an egg! Mr. Taylor sure did have a way of keeping stories interesting.

"Batter, batter, *pancake* batter!"

That was for Jason's benefit. Jason was at bat, standing at home plate waiting for a pitch. Jason frowned as he stared out at Justin. Why did they have to keep teasing him? He waved his bat. "Come on," he said. "Give me your best fastball."

Justin wound up and threw.

"Stee-rike one!" yelled Oliver, behind the catcher. He loved to be the umpire.

Personally, Jason thought the pitch was a little high, and he would have called it a ball. But he never argued with the ump. He waved his bat again and put on his game face, waiting for another pitch.

"Here comes a smoothie," Justin called, as he wound up. "Get it? Like, a mango smoothie that you whip up in the blender?"

"Just throw the ball." Jason was getting madder by the minute. "Come on, Justin!"

Justin threw.

Jason connected.

"Whoa!" shouted Oliver as the ball sailed over the head of the center fielder.

Jason circled the bases and collected high fives at home.

Maybe Dad was right after all. Baseball really *could* be fun.

Justin struck out the next three batters, and Jason's team grabbed their mitts and charged into the field.

"Go, Molly!" Jason yelled from first base, his usual position. Molly, on the pitcher's mound, was probably one of the shyest girls in school. But everybody had recently found out that she also happened to be an awesome athlete. Basketball was really her sport, but it turned out she wasn't a bad pitcher, either.

Jason saw Molly's face turn red. She loved to play, but she hated to be the center of attention. He was sorry he'd yelled her name. He would try not to do that again. "Go, Molly," he whispered under his breath.

A big fifth-grader Jason didn't know ambled up to home plate and stood swinging his bat. "Whatcha got?" he called out to Molly.

Molly didn't answer. She just squinched her eyes shut, took a deep breath, wound up, and let loose with an amazing curveball.

"Stee-rike!" yelled Oliver.

The batter looked stunned. Then he shouldered his bat again. "Okay, let's try that again," he said gamely.

Molly threw a changeup.

"Stee-rike two!"

Now the batter was blushing. He looked over at his team's bench. Jason knew he was probably embarrassed about getting struck out by a girl. Then he swung his bat a few times and shouldered it again. "Ready," he said.

Molly threw a fastball.

The boy swung hard in a desperate attempt to connect. He got a corner of the ball and hit a hard grounder right toward Jason. Jason took three easy steps, scooped up the ball, and tossed it to Molly, who had dashed over to cover first base.

"Yer out!" yelled Oliver from home base.

Jason gave Molly a thump on the shoulder. "Good work!"

Molly blushed. "Thanks," she said, as she jogged back to the mound.

Jason was having such a good time playing ball that he forgot all about Duncan and Doc and Pete. He even forgot about how much he'd *rather* be at J.J.'s — until the seventh inning, when Jennifer ran up to him while he was waiting for his turn at bat.

"Jase!" She was panting. "You have to come with me!"

Jason stared at her. "But we just tied the score!" he said.

She grabbed his hand. "Come on!" she said. "Dad needs you!"

In the Weeds

You made it! Fantastic!" When Jason walked into the kitchen, his father greeted him by tossing him a white chef's jacket. "Put this on and get to work." The kitchen of J.J.'s was steamy and hot after the fresh outdoor air. Pots boiled on the stove and the grill was smoking. Jason's father pulled a tray of bread out of the oven and kicked the door shut as he turned to the next task.

"What's up?" Jason asked as he pulled on the jacket, buttoned it, and rolled up the way-too-long sleeves.

"George had a family emergency," Dad said quickly, tossing a lump of butter into a pan on the stove. "Had to leave. We're shorthanded — and the place is completely booked tonight!"

"It's already filling up," Jason agreed. He had

counted at least seven tables full of people as he walked through the dining room.

"Tell me about it," said his dad. "We're gonna be in the weeds any minute. So, do you mind helping? I hate to ask, but —"

"I don't mind at all!" Jason knew that "in the weeds" was restaurant talk for being completely overwhelmed. And he knew his dad wouldn't ask unless he was desperate. He looked around the kitchen. "What do you want me to do first? How about if I peel those potatoes?" A small mountain of potatoes filled a bin near the sink.

"Excellent." Dad whirled around and tossed the handful of herbs he'd just chopped into a simmering pot of soup.

Jason sat down on a stool and started to peel potatoes the extra-quick way George had taught him, piling the finished ones in the sink to be rinsed before Dad cut them up into French fries.

"Ordering!" Melissa poked her head into the kitchen.

Jason was relieved to see her. Melissa was the

best waitress they had. She would help keep the night from being a total disaster. He gave her a little wave and she winked at him.

"Two onion soups, the chicken special, and a steak, well done," Melissa called out.

Dad nodded. "Okay, and you can pick up the apps for table two." He pointed at four plates on the pass-through, the shelf with a warming light where chefs put the food that was ready to go out to the dining room. "Should I fire table five?"

Jason knew that "apps" were appetizers, and that table two was the four-top (that meant it seated four people) near the restaurant's front window. He even knew that when his dad asked if he should "fire" table five he wasn't talking about telling them they were out of a job — he was asking if they were done with their appetizers so he could get their dinners ready to send out. Jason smiled to himself. He had a feeling he could even do Melissa's job if he had to. There wasn't much about J.J.'s that he didn't know.

Jason settled onto his stool and raced through the rest of the potatoes. He felt completely at home, and completely happy, amid the hustle and bustle of the kitchen. His dad banged pots and pans as he raced around the kitchen. The dishwasher, Johnny, was barely keeping up with the pile of empty plates that were already streaming in from the dining room, carried in big gray tubs by Steve, the busboy. And Melissa and the other waitstaff kept pushing open the doors to the kitchen and calling out orders. Jason could smell onion soup and sizzling meat and tomato sauce and all the other delicious smells that made this kitchen his favorite place in the world.

"Done!" Jason tossed the last potato into the sink, then stood up and wiped his hands on a kitchen towel. "What's next?"

"Salad prep." Dad pointed to the spot where George usually had all the salad stuff ready. Lettuce in one bin, tomatoes in another, cucumbers in another. The waiters and waitresses could put together plates of salad in no time — as long as everything was ready. Almost every customer got a salad, so there had to be lots of ingredients ready and waiting. But clearly, George had left before he could finish that particular job. The lettuce bin was nearly empty, and a crate of leafy greens stood waiting to be prepared.

Jason stifled a groan. Potatoes were boring enough. Washing twenty heads of lettuce and tearing them into little pieces was *not* the most fun job in the kitchen. But he knew his dad would never let him do what he *really* wanted to do: work the grill. Dad always said he was way too young to be around all that heat and sizzle. But Jason longed to do George's job, tossing food on the big grill and cooking it perfectly for each customer. Medium rare steak? No problem. Grilled zucchini for a vegetarian? Got it! Extra-big cheeseburger for Gary, a regular customer? Coming right up!

But Jason knew that in a restaurant kitchen, every job was important. Keeping the customers happy was the first order of business, no matter what. And since his dad had a lot more experience at the grill, Jason knew that he could help most by doing other things.

Jason pulled the first head of lettuce out of the crate. He would happily do whatever Dad asked him to do. The head chef in a kitchen (that would be Dad) was like the captain on a ship. You followed his orders no matter what. If everyone did what they were told, the ship would stay on course. If they didn't, all hands would go down with the ship!

After the lettuce, Jason cut long loaves of crusty bread into slices for the breadbaskets that went to each table. He fetched a dozen lemons, three pork chops, and a bunch of parsley from the walk-in refrigerator. He pitched in to help Johnny scrub pots. He even put on a busboy's jacket and helped Steve clear tables so that they could be set again for the next customers, who were already waiting to sit down.

"Eighty-six on the chicken special!" shouted Jason's dad. Jason grabbed a piece of chalk and added "Chix" to the eighty-six board. When the waiters and waitresses saw it, they would know the kitchen was all out of that menu item.

Finally, the endless stream of orders slowed to a trickle. The noise in the kitchen died down enough so that Jason could hear the Beatles, his dad's favorite music to cook by. Melissa and the other waitstaff began to count their tips, polish silverware, and set up their stations for the next night.

"Whew!" Dad said, wiping his forehead with a kitchen towel. "Never thought I'd see the end of that rush!" He grinned at Jason. "You saved my skin tonight, buddy."

Jason grinned back.

"Hey, you must be starving!" Dad said. He hardly ever got hungry while he was working, and usually forgot to eat until he came home.

Suddenly, Jason realized that his stomach was growling. "Can I make us something on the grill?" he asked.

Dad hesitated. Then he smiled. "You bet." He handed Jason the spatula. "Go to it."

By the time Melissa flipped the sign on the front door to read CLOSED, Jason had put together a big platter full of his latest version of the Amazin'

Jason. The whole crew sat down to eat as they replayed their crazy night.

"Excellent sandwich," said Melissa, as she finished the last bite. "I love the bacon. It's perfect! You're going to be a cook just like your dad, aren't you?"

Jason smiled. "Def —" he began, but his father interrupted him.

"No!" Dad folded his arms across his chest. "Jason's destined for better things than slaving away in a hot kitchen!"

Jason pushed his chair away from the table. Was that the way his dad thanked him, after all the work he had done? "I have homework to do," he said shortly. And he left without saying good-bye.

Off for the Pole

[S]omebody's in a good mood." Mr. Taylor smiled as he walked by. Jason was looking through his cubby, trying to find his math notebook. He was humming "Good Day Sunshine," a Beatles tune he'd heard the night before at J.J.'s.

It was true. Jason *was* in a good mood, even though his dad still did not seem to understand how much he loved to cook. The night at the restaurant had been so much fun! And Jason felt great about being able to help out. Someday, somehow, he would convince his dad that he belonged in the restaurant business.

"Maybe that's because Duncan found his baseball," Jason said to Mr. Taylor. It felt like ages since the last time the class had sat in the reading corner, listening to Duncan's story. But Jason had been thinking about it the whole time: while he was peeling potatoes, while he was clearing tables, and even while he was making sandwiches at the grill. He could just picture Duncan catching Pete the penguin in the act of treating his prized baseball like an egg.

"Wasn't that a relief?" Mr. Taylor asked with a grin.

"What happens next?" Jason asked. By now, he was sitting at his desk, watching Mr. Taylor shuffle papers.

"Well, I guess it's about time we found out, isn't it?" Mr. Taylor led the class over to the reading corner, turned on the light, and folded himself into his big green chair.

Duncan felt a lot better once he had found his baseball. He gave Pete quite a lecture about taking other people's property, not that Pete seemed to understand a word he said. The little bird just stood there, craning his neck, flapping his wings, and squawking until Doc picked him up and put him to bed.

That night when he went to sleep, Duncan made sure that the ball was deep inside his sleeping bag, where Pete couldn't find it. He couldn't risk having the ball disappear again, not when it was time to head for the North Pole!

For that's where they were going — the very next day. When Duncan woke up, he saw that his father was already up and packing. Doc muttered to himself as he added tools to a pouch. "Better bring the magnets," Duncan heard Doc say. "And the vise grips." Pete watched closely, cocking his head thoughtfully.

Duncan packed the last of his things into a duffel bag and placed the ball carefully on top before he zipped it up.

The mess tent was noisy and busy as the expedition members stocked up on pancakes with lots of maple syrup. As he was finishing his third plateful, Duncan looked up to see Dave, the cook, smiling down at him. "Got a going-away present," Dave said. He held out an orange. It wasn't big, and it was slightly wrinkled looking, but it was an orange. "It's the last one. The crew would kill me if they knew I was giving it away. They don't get much fresh fruit up here."

"But why are you giving it to me, then?" Duncan asked.

"It's not for you." Dave rolled the orange down the table to where Pete was sitting with Doc. "It's for the little guy. He wants an egg so bad. Maybe this will keep him away from your ball."

Duncan grinned as he watched Pete nuzzle the orange, making soft squawking noises as he examined it closely. It was true. The penguin just wanted something to take care of. "Great idea. Thanks!"

The mess tent was emptying out. Duncan knew what that meant. It was time to get going. They would be taking five dog sleds to the North Pole, and Duncan was going to be driving his very own team! He had met the dogs and had some basic training the day before, and Stan seemed to think he was ready. "Nothing to it," he'd said. "Just tell 'em 'git up' to get going, 'gee' to turn right, and 'haw' to turn left. You'll be following the other sleds, anyway, so your main job is just going to be to hold on tight."

Stan wasn't kidding. Duncan found that out as soon as his dogs took off, barking madly and towing his sled behind them. Duncan ran alongside the sled, helping to steer it and making sure that nothing fell off. That included Pete, who was riding with Duncan since Doc's sled was loaded with tools. Pete sat upright, staring off in the distance and squawking softly. Once in a while Duncan jumped on and rode for a little bit, watching the vast white world of ice and snow unfold before his eyes.

Duncan was proud of the way his dog team kept up with the others. Even though he was last in line, he had a good view of Doc in front of him. "Good going, Martha!" he yelled to his lead dog. "Keep it up, Max!" he shouted to the wheel dog, the one who helped keep the sled steered in the right direction.

There was no wind, and the sky was a clear wash of bright blue. Duncan was cold, but happy. He looked forward to setting up camp on the ice that afternoon and comparing notes with Doc and the rest of the expedition members. They would be traveling together for many days before they reached the North Pole. If the weather stayed this calm, the trip was going to be a breeze.

Wham! Suddenly, Duncan felt the sled lean way up on its side. He jumped off just in time to see its runners scraping on a huge pressure ridge, a mound formed by moving ice. Duncan had read all about pressure ridges, but he hadn't seen this one coming.

The sled tipped up even higher. "Stop!" Duncan yelled to the dogs. "Stop!"

Martha obeyed, pulling up short and forcing the whole team to come to a halt.

But it was too late.

The sled had tipped all the way onto its side, and both runners were well off the ice. Pete had jumped off the sled in the nick of time, and he stood squawking and flapping as he and Duncan watched all their food, gear, and clothing fly onto the ice. Pete's orange bumped off the sled, rolled straight into a crevasse, and disappeared without a trace.

Duncan felt his stomach lurch as he watched his duffel bag land hard and burst open. "No!" he yelled, as he watched his precious baseball roll away, its red seams and black signatures the only things that made it visible against the snow. Would it follow the orange into the bottomless crack in the ice?

Pete moved faster than Duncan had ever seen him move, first waddling and then flopping down onto his belly to slide toward the ball.

"Go, Pete!" yelled Duncan. The penguin must think he was rescuing his beloved egg. Who cared, as long as he saved Duncan's treasure from being lost forever?

The ball skipped across the snow, and Pete slid after it. He had just about caught up to it, too! Then, suddenly, Duncan saw something huge and white looming up from behind a pressure ridge.

Duncan felt a chill run up his spine as he watched the giant creature stalk slowly and directly toward Pete. The penguin was about to meet one of the most frightening predators on earth.

A polar bear.

Doc Does His Best

Immediately, Duncan realized something. Seeing a polar bear — a real, live, living, breathing, enormous, humongous polar bear — was a lot different from *reading* about polar bears.

Duncan stood frozen in place.

Meanwhile, Pete stood up and prepared to take another slide. The little penguin didn't seem to have the least idea that he was being stalked by a huge, terrifying beast.

Was Pete about to become a penguin-burger, right in front of Duncan's eyes? Sure, the little penguin might be a bit of a pest at times, but in a funny way Duncan had come to care for him. It was almost as if Pete was the little brother Duncan had always wished for. A pesky little brother, for sure. But Duncan was most definitely not interested in watching Pete get eaten.

Even worse, what if the bear considered Pete nothing but an appetizer? It wouldn't be long before he was looking for his main course — and Duncan would be the first thing he spotted.

Duncan had been in more than one very sticky situation in the course of his young life, but this was, without a doubt, the stickiest ever.

If he did nothing, the polar bear would most likely eat Pete within the next few seconds.

On the other hand, what could he do? The tranquilizer gun that was strapped to his sled had been thrown off with everything else, and now it was buried within the tumble of objects that lay scattered on the snow. So Duncan could not shoot the bear. All he could do was — what? Yell? Shake his fist at the bear? Ask it politely to please leave them alone?

It was like being stuck in a bad dream, the kind where you see something horrible happening and you can't do a thing about it.

Suddenly, Pete let out a loud squawk. Finally, he'd seen the bear! His tiny eyes seemed to grow large and his beak opened wide as he squawked again and again, shrieking in fear.

It didn't seem to matter that Pete had never seen a polar bear before. The penguin knew exactly what he was facing. And he was *terrified*.

Duncan clenched his fists and opened his mouth to yell.

Not a sound came out.

He started to run toward Pete and the bear.

Then . . . "Get down!" someone shouted. "Drop, Duncan!"

Duncan dropped.

A shot rang out.

Duncan squeezed his eyes shut, then opened them, hoping to see the polar bear stopped in its tracks.

But the bear was still moving — straight toward Pete and Duncan.

Duncan looked back to see who had fired the shot. "Dad!" Doc was standing twenty paces behind him, a tranquilizer gun held in the ready-aim-fire position. "Where did you come from?"

Doc let the gun fall to his waist. He considered the question. "Well, I suppose from the north," he said, "since I was out ahead of you."

"I meant —" Duncan realized that there was no time to chat. "Never mind. What about that bear?"

They both turned to see that the great white bear was only yards away from Pete.

Pete gave one last, hopeless squawk as the bear took its final steps toward him.

Doc shouldered the gun and took careful aim.

He shot again.

The bear didn't even pause. He just kept coming.

Amazin' But True

Um, Mr. Taylor?"

A boy named Tim from the class down the hall was standing in the classroom doorway.

"What is it, Tim?"

"Ms. Peabody says to tell you that the bell rang. School's over. The buses are waiting."

Mr. Taylor raised a bushy eyebrow. "Well, that's a first." He laughed. "I guess we were kind of caught up in our story. Thanks, Tim."

Tim paused for a second. Jason could tell he had heard about Mr. Taylor's stories. Everybody envied the kids in class 3B. What other teacher told such good stories? Or any stories at all, for that matter?

Mr. Taylor unfolded himself from his chair and turned off the light. "That's all, folks!"

"You mean we have to wait until tomorrow to

find out what happens to Duncan and Pete?" Jason could not believe it. How was he supposed to sleep that night, not knowing?

Mr. Taylor shrugged. "I'll be in mighty big trouble if you all miss your buses."

Jason opened his mouth. He was about to say he didn't care about any bus, since he always walked home. Then he stopped himself. Obviously, Mr. Taylor couldn't keep the whole class after school just for a story.

"We'll finish up tomorrow," Mr. Taylor said. He crossed his heart. "I promise. Now, let's hustle!"

Everybody jumped up and ran to their cubbies to grab their jackets and backpacks. "Are you going to play today?" Molly asked Jason. She was stuffing a well-oiled baseball glove into her pack.

Jason shook his head. "Nope. Maybe tomorrow." He was headed for J.J.'s. If George was out again, his dad would need him.

But George wasn't out. When Jason walked into the kitchen, George put down his spatula and gave him a big high five. "You're the man!"

he said. "Thanks for covering for me. I heard you did great."

Jason blushed and shrugged, but he felt all warm inside. If George had heard about it, that meant maybe his dad had boasted about how helpful Jason had been.

"Yeah, Melissa couldn't say enough about you," George went on. "She said you were a real cool customer, never lost your head even when things were really hopping."

Melissa. Jason should have known. His dad wouldn't have been the one to brag. He didn't even *want* Jason in the kitchen.

George looked closely at Jason. "Something wrong, chief?" he asked.

Jason shook his head.

"Hungry?" George asked, pointing to the grill. "I've got a grilled cheese with your name on it."

Jason shook his head again. "No, thanks. I think I'll go see if Dad needs any help." He walked further into the kitchen and spotted his dad bent over the giant mixer, pouring a ten-pound bag of flour into its bowl.

"Making pizza dough?" Jason knew J.J.'s always served pizza on Thursdays.

Dad straightened up. "Second batch," he said. "The first one didn't rise right."

"I wonder if the yeast was too old." Jason peered into the mixing bowl. "Or maybe the temperature wasn't quite right. George said that the oven has been acting up lately."

"Either way, I think it'll work this time." Dad turned on the mixer, and the giant paddle started turning and folding the flour and water into a big, gooey mass of dough. Jason watched happily. Ever since he was about three years old, he'd loved watching that giant mixer. He could remember when he had to stand on tiptoe to see inside the big bowl.

"How was school?" Dad was already on to the next task, grating mozzarella cheese for the pizza topping.

"Fine." Jason would have loved to tell his dad all about Duncan and Doc and Pete and their trip to the North Pole, but he knew there was no way his dad had time right now to listen to all of that.

"So, what can I do?" He picked up an onion. "Want me to peel a bunch of these?"

Dad put down the grater. "Jason."

"What?"

"Don't you have something better to do? Something you'd *rather* do?"

Jason met his father's eyes. "No, I don't. There is nothing I would rather be doing right this minute than be in this kitchen, working with you." How much clearer could he be?

"You really mean that, don't you?" asked his father, looking at Jason intently.

"I really mean that."

"Tell you what, then." Dad stopped looking quite so serious. "I'm starving, and I'm sure George is, too. How about whipping up a batch of those — what do you call that excellent sandwich you invented?"

"The Amazin' Jason."

"Great name." Dad picked up his grater again. "As a matter of fact," he said, as Jason headed toward the grill, "I think I'm going to put that sandwich on the menu. Okay with you?"

Jason felt like he had just hit a grand slam. "That is absolutely, positively, *definitely* okay with me."

"I think we should do some product testing first, though." Dad sounded thoughtful.

"What do you mean?"

"We need to see what the public thinks of the sandwich. Like, how would your typical third-grader like it?" Now Dad's eyes were twinkling.

Jason still didn't get it. "But how would we find *that* out?"

"Special Snack!" said Dad.

Jason stared at him. Special Snack was when a parent brought a treat to class for everyone to share. Sometimes it was cupcakes on somebody's birthday. Or sometimes it was a kind of food nobody had ever tasted before, like when Oliver and his mom brought red bean candy during the class unit on Japan.

On the one hand, it was so totally cool that Dad liked the Amazin' Jason enough to A: put it on the menu, and B: serve it for Special Snack.

On the other hand, there was just one teeny problem.

If Dad brought Amazin' Jasons to class and told everybody who had invented the sandwich, the teasing would never end.

Saved

Jason could not figure out how to say no to his father. After all, how could he explain that he was embarrassed about liking to cook? His dad would think he was ashamed, and that was the *last* thing Jason wanted — especially now that Dad had finally started to understand how much he loved working at J.J.'s.

So he didn't say a thing except, "Great!" And at eleven o'clock the next morning, Jason's and Jennifer's father came to Mr. Taylor's class.

"That's your *dad*?" Leo asked, when he saw Jason's dad walk in. Mr. Tourville was wearing a bright white, starched jacket. He was carrying a stack of big metal trays covered with foil.

Jason nodded. "He's a chef."

"I guess I knew your family owned a restaurant,

but I never really thought about who did the cooking," Leo said.

While he waited to hear what Leo would say next, Jason reminded himself of what he had decided the night before, while he was lying in bed trying to sleep. He had decided that he was *proud* of being a good cook. He happened to know that many of the best cooks in the world were men. Besides, what was more important than feeding people food that was healthy and delicious? People needed food to survive. But they needed it to be happy, too. Jason thought about all the great things his dad cooked: awesome pancakes for Sunday breakfast, chicken soup when anyone had a cold, the best ribs in the world for the annual Fourth of July Tourville family reunion. Dad's food made people feel good.

Whoops! Leo was still talking. "— so cool! I always wanted to learn how to make really good spaghetti sauce. Do you think your dad could teach me?"

Jason looked at him. "*I* could teach you," he said.

Just then, Jason's father peeled the foil off the top of the trays. "Oohh!" A delicious smell filled room 3B. Everybody clustered around to see where it came from.

"Yum!" Mr. Taylor's eyes lit up when he saw the sandwiches.

"It's a sandwich called the Amazin' Jason." Jennifer started talking before Jason could say a word. "Jason made it up. It has cheese, bacon —"

"Jennifer!" Their dad put a hand on her shoulder. "Let Jason tell."

Jason felt himself blushing. But he stepped forward. "Jennifer had most of it," he said. "Cheese, bacon, onion, mustard — and two secret ingredients." Even Dad and George didn't know what those ingredients were. Not yet.

Cricket was already holding out a paper plate. "Can I have one?" she asked.

Jason took the spatula his dad handed him and started serving sandwiches.

Jennifer uncovered the other tray. "We have

plain cheese sandwiches, too, in case anybody doesn't like bacon or onions."

Jennifer sounded like she'd made the food herself, but Jason didn't care. So what if this was the first time she had ever seemed excited about being part of J.J.'s? He just kept serving sandwiches.

"Man, Jason, these are good." Leo had jumped back in line as soon as he'd finished his sandwich. Now he was holding out his plate for another serving. "Justin and Daniel are dopes for teasing you. Wait'll I tell them what they're missing!"

"Can I have seconds?" Mr. Taylor was back for more, too.

Jason grinned at him. "Only if you promise to tell us what happened next."

"I'll be glad to. And we happen to have some time right now, before math." Mr. Taylor turned to Mr. Tourville. "Care to stay?"

"Sure!" Jason's dad unbuttoned his chef's coat and joined the class as they followed Mr. Taylor to the reading corner, paper plates in hand. "Jason and Jennifer told us some of the story last night, so I won't be totally lost. As I recall, the last thing we heard was that Pete the penguin was about to get eaten by a polar bear."

"Very good!" said Mr. Taylor. "But Duncan's father has just turned up, so we're hoping for the best, right?"

"Right!" everybody yelled.

Jason thought it was funny to see Dad sitting cross-legged on the floor with everybody else. Funny, but nice. They smiled at each other as Mr. Taylor turned on the light and began.

The polar bear was reaching out a huge paw toward Pete when another shot rang out. The paw dropped — and Pete finally unfroze and ran toward Doc and Duncan.

"Blistering Ballistics! I got him!" Doc held the shotgun high in the air and shook it as Duncan watched the polar bear slowly slump onto the snow. "Just call me Old Eagle-Eye!"

Pete tottered up to Duncan and Doc, and Doc patted the penguin on the head. "I could never have forgiven myself if I brought you all the way to the North Pole only to get eaten by a polar bear!"

Then he turned to his son. "But most importantly, *you're* okay." Doc wrapped his arms around Duncan. Duncan felt safe and loved and protected, just like when he was little and Doc would wrap him up in a warm, dry towel after his bath. Suddenly, Duncan knew that no matter what, Doc would always be there for him. He hugged Doc back. "Daddy," he murmured into his father's broad chest.

Then he stepped back. "But — is the bear going to be okay?" Duncan couldn't help feeling bad for the huge creature. A minute ago it had looked like the king of the Arctic. Now it looked like a pile of dirty white shag rugs.

"Sure!" Doc waved a hand. "He'll wake up in a few hours with a bad headache, that's all."

"So he's definitely asleep for now?" Duncan took a few steps closer to the bear and saw that its eyes were tightly closed and that it was breathing long, slow breaths. Then he tiptoed past the sleeping giant and plucked his baseball from the spot where it had stopped rolling. He held it tightly in his mittened hands, reading the names: Bill Mueller. David Ortiz. Ellis Burks. Then he shoved it deep inside the pocket of his parka.

"Thanks, Dad." He gave his dad another hug. "I mean it. Thanks." Maybe Doc couldn't remember to tie his own shoes some days, but when it had really mattered, Duncan's dad had come through like a hero. "You saved me."

"Of course!" Doc looked surprised. "I would never let anything happen to you, son." He hugged Duncan back. "Thundering Typhoons! We're a team. And we're on our way to the North Pole!"

Mr. Taylor leaned back in his chair and let out a big yawn, stretching his arms wide. "That's about it!" he said.

"What?" Jason couldn't believe his ears.

Mr. Taylor shrugged. "There's not much more to tell. They made it to the North Pole, which ended up looking pretty much exactly the same as all the other ice and snow they'd traveled across. And they made it back with no other real trouble. Duncan held on to that ball, and as far as I know, he still has it. And he and Doc still travel all over the world. I think by now that's the only Red Sox ball that's been on all seven continents and to both Poles."

"But — but what about the McTeagleometer at the North Pole? The one they went to fix?" Oliver looked very concerned.

"Funny thing about that." Mr. Taylor laughed a little. "The thing wasn't even broken! All Doc did was tap it with a screwdriver, and it started working perfectly. After that, there wasn't anything for Duncan and Doc to do but head home."

"Did Pete stay at the North Pole?" Cricket asked.

"Oh, no. They took him back to Boston, where he'd be safe." Mr. Taylor raised his bushy eyebrows. "Any other questions?"

Jason bit his lip. When he had first made up his list of items for a Taylor-Made Tale, he had thought it would be really cool if he could stump Mr. Taylor. But now, he wasn't so sure. Maybe Mr. Taylor had gotten close enough to meeting the Ultimate Challenge. After all, he had fit in the quicksand, the penguin, the polar bear, and the baseball. So what if he'd forgotten one item? Jason did not really want to be the one to bring it up.

But good old Jennifer did it for him. "Mr. Taylor, you forgot all about the cactus!"

The End

Jason sucked in a breath and looked over at his dad. Why did Jennifer always have to be such a loudmouth? Mr. Taylor's story had been great, even if it didn't include a cactus. So he hadn't met the Ultimate Challenge. So what? Jason could hardly stand to look at Mr. Taylor. The poor guy. Why couldn't Jennifer just let it go?

But when he did look, Mr. Taylor was smiling. "Ha!" he said. "Funny you should say that. The fact is, Duncan and Doc forgot all about the cactus, too."

Their first stop when they returned to Boston was the zoo, of course. It wasn't easy to say good-bye to Pete. For a second, Duncan even thought of begging Doc to take Pete home with them. Maybe he could live in the bathtub again! But then he remembered that they were hardly ever home.

And it wasn't like they could take Pete along if they had to go to, say, the Sahara. Pete's feet would not like the hot sand.

"You'll be happier here," Duncan told the little bird. He and Doc each gave him a hug just before they handed him over to the keeper.

Pete squawked and flapped a wing at Duncan and Doc. Then the keeper gave him a little fish out of the bucket she carried, and Pete turned to wad-dle after her into the penguin house. He stopped once to glance back at Doc and let out a loving squawk. But then he followed the fish.

Duncan and Doc were both quiet as the taxi took them the rest of the way home. "Well, here we are again," Doc said, as he unlocked the door to their apartment. He put down his duffel bag and began to sort through the huge pile of mail that had been pushed through the slot in the door.

"Oh, no!" Duncan slapped his head. "I don't believe it."

"Something wrong?" Doc wasn't really paying attention. He slit open a big envelope and stared at the letter inside.

"I forgot to give Theodore the note about watering the plants!" The note he'd written so carefully was lying in plain sight on the table in the front hall.

"Oh, well." Doc didn't seem concerned. "That's the beauty of the plants we've chosen, isn't it? They can go without water *forever*, practically."

As he began to look around the apartment, Duncan had to admit that his father was right. Every single plant they owned looked just fine — because they were all cacti. Spiny, green cacti in every size and shape, from teeny marble-sized ones to the saguaro, whose long arms nearly reached the ceiling. But every one of them was able to go for months without water. The prickly pear near the window even looked like it was about to bloom! Duncan would give them each a good soaking that night, and all would be well. It was wonderful to be home.

"Get out your lists!" Doc waved the letter at Duncan. "It's time to start planning another trip."

Duncan sighed. Oh, well. It was good to travel, too. "Where are we going?"

"Ever hear of Tuva?" Doc was smiling.

"Nope." Duncan smiled back.

"Well, I'm sure it's a very interesting place. We'll read all about it at the library tomorrow." Doc put down the letter and gave Duncan a big hug. "For now, let's order some pizza, shall we?"

And that's exactly what they did.

After a moment, Mr. Taylor reached up and turned off the lamp. "That's it!"

Jason looked around the classroom. His eye fell on a plant in a bright yellow pot. The prickly round cactus had been on Mr. Taylor's desk ever since the first day of school. "Um, Mr. Taylor?" he asked. "Just out of curiosity, where did you get that cactus?"

Mr. Taylor smiled. "From some friends who lived downstairs from my apartment in Boston." His eyes were twinkling. "They went away a lot, and I always took care of their plants. When they remembered to ask, that is!"